See the Ocean

Published by Ideals Children's Books
An imprint of Hambleton-Hill Publishing, Inc.
Nashville, Tennessee 37218

Printed and bound in Mexico

Library of Congress Cataloging-in-Publication Data
Condra, Estelle, 1944–
    See the ocean / by Estelle Condra ; illustrated by Linda Crockett-
Blassingame.
        p.   cm.
    Summary: Driving through mountain fog to the beach, two young
brothers compete to see who will catch the first glimpse of the
ocean, but it is their blind sister Nellie who senses it first.
    ISBN 1-57102-005-5
    [1. Seashore—Fiction. 2. Blind—Fiction. 3. Physically handi-
capped—Fiction. 4. Family life—Fiction.] I. Crockett-Blassingame,
Linda, 1948– ill. II. Title.
PZ7.C75916Se   1994
[E]—dc20   94-4234

CIP
                                                    AC

First Edition

10 9 8 7 6 5 4 3 2 1

To my parents, Kate and Ferrie, who taught me to see with my mind.
                                                    —E.C.

The illustrations in this book were rendered in oils.
The display type and text are set in Sabon.
Color separations were made by Wisconsin Technicolor.
Printed and bound by R.R. Donnelley.

See the Ocean

By Estelle Condra
Illustrated by Linda Crockett-Blassingame

Ideals Children's Books • Nashville, Tennessee

Nellie loved the ocean. She loved going
to the beach with her parents and her
two older brothers, Gerald and Jamin.
Once a year Nellie's family took the long
road that led through the flat desert
plains and across the Black Mountains
to their beach house at the ocean.

When she was a baby, they dug a
small round dam for Nellie in the sand.
She lay cooing in the cool water that
came and went. She fingered the grainy
sand and kicked and wiggled her toes in
the shallow waves that washed into her
dam. She never cried when the saltwater
stung her eyes or when she got sand in
her mouth.

Gerald and Jamin brought tiny fish in their red and yellow sand pails to Nellie. They collected shells and seaweed and pieces of driftwood for her to touch. Her mother made a beard and eyebrows from sea foam on Nellie's face, and her father carried her high on his shoulders into the surf.

Nellie took her first steps on the beach. She waddled around in a striped bathing suit, stepping on a sandcastle here and slipping and rolling in a sand ditch there. Her skin tanned as brown as the rocks and her hair bleached as white as sea foam. She fed crumbs to the squawking sea gulls. She tossed pebbles in a pool between the rocks, and she laughed at the sound. She hummed and babbled her baby babble into the wind.

When she could talk, she asked
endless questions about the ocean. "How
old is it? How big? How deep? What's
the color? Why the waves? Why the
sound?" Her father answered as well as
he could, and her mother explained with
stories.

Each year they loaded their car and
set out along the road that led through
the flat desert plains and across the high
Black Mountains to the ocean where
they had their beach house. Nellie never
fought with her brothers for a window
seat. She sat happily between them in
the backseat, dressing and undressing
her doll and listening. She listened to
them talking and telling about the things
they passed along the road.

They played games to while away the hours of their long journey. Nellie never played. First, she was too young. Later, she wanted to be the scorekeeper. She kept the score in her head, always knowing who won and who lost and by how many points.

Every year when they reached the foothills of the Black Mountains, another game started as they drove up the mountain pass. Gerald and Jamin leaned forward and stretched their necks and tried to be the first to see the ocean from the top of the mountain—just a glimpse of the shiny water far below them counted.

Sometimes Gerald would be the first
one to shout out, "There it is, shining
blue between those trees down there."
Other times Jamin would be the one to
yell first, "There! There are white caps!
That means wind on the ocean." Nellie
never competed. She just sat quietly,
listening to the talk and excitement and
feeling excited herself.

One year as they were driving up the mountain pass, a heavy mist blew in. When they came to the top of the mountain, the mist lay thick around them and across the mountain peaks. It covered the valleys below as far as the eyes could see. No one could see the ocean.

But then a soft, salty breeze crept up the mountain and through the open window, brushing over Nellie's cheek and whispering in her ear, and suddenly she said, "I see it!"

"No fair, Mother! She can't," complained Jamin.

"No one can see it from here today," Gerald joined in.

"But I do, I do," insisted Nellie.

"She's cheating! She can't see it!" complained the boys.

"If she sees it, let her tell us what it looks like," said their father.

Slowly Nellie started. "The ocean is an old, old man born at the beginning of time. He breathes a loud, salty breath, and his beard blows white on the sandy beach. Fish swim in his long, wavy hair. On his head he wears a crown of pearls. On his feet he wears shoes of shells.

"Sometimes the wind blows his hair about in big wild waves. Then he gets angry, and he roars and hisses and spits. When the sun shines, he laughs and gurgles and prattles in the rock pools. He smiles a wide silver and green smile on the beach. On his shoulders he carries ships and boats.

"But at night he's more beautiful than ever. At night he wears a dark, silvery gray cloak with moons and stars sprinkled upon it. Every night before he goes to sleep, he pulls a soft, misty blanket over himself."

For a long while, no one spoke. They just looked and looked at Nellie. Then Nellie's mother turned around in her seat and stroked Nellie's cheek.

Jamin grumbled, "It's still not fair."

"How could she see through the mist when we can't? She can't even see!" said Gerald.

"Now boys, stop that," said their father in a thick voice.

And their mother said, "Listen and pay attention. Though your sister's eyes are blind, she can see with her mind."

Nellie smiled to herself as she thought how very
much she loved the ocean.